T0104938

Set Your Compass to the Stars Anthology 2012

ANTOINETTE V. FRANKLIN

authorHOUSE®

AuthorHouse™
1663 Liberty Drive
Bloomington, IN 47403
www.authorhouse.com
Phone: 1-800-839-8640

© 2013 Antoinette V. Franklin. All rights reserved.

No part of this book may be reproduced, stored in a retrieval system, or transmitted by any means without the written permission of the author.

Published by AuthorHouse   03/07/2013

ISBN: 978-1-4772-9802-2 (sc)
ISBN: 978-1-4772-9803-9 (e)

Library of Congress Control Number: 2012923532

Any people depicted in stock imagery provided by Thinkstock are models, and such images are being used for illustrative purposes only. Certain stock imagery © Thinkstock.

This book is printed on acid-free paper.

Because of the dynamic nature of the Internet, any web addresses or links contained in this book may have changed since publication and may no longer be valid. The views expressed in this work are solely those of the author and do not necessarily reflect the views of the publisher, and the publisher hereby disclaims any responsibility for them.

DEDICATION

Dedicated to the memory of Dr. Carter G. Woodson, founder of Black History Week in 1926. "This celebration and remembrance would later evolve into Black History Month now African American Heritage Month." We thank Dr. Woodson for preserving the legacy of our people. A Native American proverb states, "We all have history."

Carter G. Woodson was born on December 19, 1875 in New Canton, VA. "He was an American historian who first opened the long-neglected field of black studies to scholars and also popularized the field in the schools and colleges of blacks.

Carter was born to a poor family. He supported himself by working in the coal mines of Kentucky and was unable to enroll in high school until he was 20. After graduating in less than two years, he taught high school, wrote articles, studied at home and abroad and received his Ph.D. From Harvard University in (1912). In 1915, he founded the Association for Study of Negro Life and History to encourage scholars to engage in the intensive study of the past as it related to Africans and their descendents throughout the world in 1915. (http:www.africanwithin.com/woodson/woodson_bio1.htm.)

Dr. Woodson served as dean of the College of Liberal Arts and head of the graduate faculty at Howard University, Washington D. C. He edited the first edition of the association's principal scholarly publication, *The Journal of Negro History*, which remains an important periodical for more than 30 years. Dr. Woodson's most important work and often widely consulted text *The Negro in Our History, The Education of the Negro Prior to 1861 and A Century of Negro Migration,* Before his death on April 3, 1950, he was working on a projected six volume Encyclopedia African. Dr. Woodson's most sought after book is *The Mis-Education of the Negro,* still raises questions about our education system such as to what and who African Americans are educated for. (http:www.africanwithin.com/woodson/woodson_bio1.htm.)

Black History was so named because, "Though the 13th Amendment to the constitution was signed in January 1863 which abolished slavery and on January 1st midnight the first watch service was held to commemorate the occasion. Some of our slave ancestors did not hear about the news of freedom until February. Texas was not officially notified until 1865 and it is written that in Texas some slave owners held slaves seven years later. This is the reason Dr. Woodson choose the month of February.

This book is also dedicated to lovers of books and those who write. We are encouraging readers to input positive thoughts into the cavities of our being and renew the spirit. We must embrace all areas of our life and learn to build a better future for our next generations of readers and writers. There are quotes sprinkled throughout to strengthen and inspire.

Carter G. Woodson

(1875 - 1950)

FOREWORD

by George Bussey

The journey through the mind's eye, rhythms, sounds and spirits of each of these artist forces us to attend to a voice that is both ours and not. It is the voice of the inner soul of one communicating on a very intimate level with another. A voice that shocks us into an awakening as if we were coming out of a deep slumber, up from the muck and mire of mindless imprisonment. It is a voice not easily heard outside of the self, but one that dramatically changes how the eyes see and the body moves after the hearing of it. Somehow this wake-up call for the spirit has opened the pathway to another universe changing who we were forever.

Some believe that the earth is an organism and that we have been put here to reflect its being. The artists are given the highest responsibility. They are part of the shamanistic tradition calling on spirits and taking from the earth what is needed for awakening and healing. The role of the artist is to keep us rooted in the reality of the moment, to shake us out of complacency, to awaken us again to reflection and meditation, to enable us to reincarnate, and as Jean Paul Marat said, "to turn ourselves inside out and see the whole world with fresh eyes."

The main question for you who have chosen to begin the voyage here is whether or not you are willing to risk looking into a mirror to witness the cracking of the outer shell of the self so that the inner core of being is only seen. A question of exposing through one's eyes the new self that has emerged from these reflections. All of which have reshaped the tone and timbre of your voice so that a new song of life is sung because you have ventured to expose yourself on the outskirts of universal being.

TABLE OF CONTENTS

POETRY PART I
WHEN WE WERE FREE

SHORT STORIES PART II
"A CHANGE IS GONNA COME"

ESSAYS PART III
WORDS TO INSPIRE

POETRY
PART I

WHEN WE WERE FREE

"Take only memories leave nothing but footprints."

Chief Seattle Native American

STARS

Photo by Rafael F.

LATE WINTER'S MOON

i remember late winter's moon,
the only moon that never spoke
just observing
with silent, sleepy eye
standing tall and pale
a good listener that saw i was troubled

instead of leaving quickly
he stayed and listened to me

i wanted to know about him and why he was so quiet
but he didn't speak as i babbled to his nods and smiles
believing he understood
though i had no idea if he understood my English

he left after our meeting, without the usual hurried exit
he stayed and listened to me
walking slowly, westward on the azure road,
back lit by the approaching sun,
spanning the thinned canopy of trees.

and i noticed, i felt a little better
what the problem was, i don't remember
maybe late winter's moon
took that burden, along with his own
so I'd never see that problem, or him, again.

2004
Cortnee Mendoza

VENGEANCE JONES IS HANDSOME

Vengeance Jones is handsome
sitting, watching the convulsive sea,
as he usually does in hope's city.

around his neck's a jade piece
old, once belonging to a Chinese princess,
according to him.

he said this with so much confidence
i could only humor him,
and his words.

because how could he, the visage of murder
with a back like gunfire
legs like rage and arms
built by vendetta
cherish properly
the placidity and astute nature of jade?

if Vengeance ever cherishes,
he cherishes like lava cherished cherry ice cream
    like chickens cherishes deep frying
    like the brain cherishes dementia.

Cortnee Mendoza

"Write what feels good."

Walter Mosley

BLUES

A back alley way
was the meeting place
for the men of music.
They played and
mourned out a song.

You couldn't taste
what ailed them
but you felt
the words of
their songs.

These blues men spoke of
bad times,
fun times,
sad endings of the shades
of what would come.

Texas blues notes
rang off concrete walls
on a summer day,
echoing off mesquite trees becoming
spiced Texan harmony
of things that would come.

Indigo blues with shades of
things to come
gathered the men
to sing
songs and harmonize
about things to come.

Let the Words Fly Creative Writing Class
March 10, 2012

Antoinette V. Franklin

LOVE IS IMPORTANT

Our God wants us to love each other.
to put someone before ourselves,
to enjoy every day
and not worry
because we have Him.

Love is important to our God.
He wants us to be bold for Him,
to tell someone everywhere
about your
Lord and Savior.

Calm down and enjoy your Life.
Stop worrying about everything.
Give it to Jesus and keep it
moving.

Our God has a plan
for you and me
love is always important.

Love Sugar,

Juanita Wilson

Let the Words Fly Creative Writing Class
3/10/2012

MY BEGINNING

My beginning, "I was born dead,"
but God had a plan.
I made it through
second and third time
I went to the light,
but the fourth time
God let me see myself
dead on a table.

God heard a prayer that
was said just for me,
and he breathed life back into me.

You never know
what God is
going to do,
but always remember
that he always has.

Always Believe,
"Sis Sugar"
Juanita Wilson

MY DREAM VACATION

Vacation,
what a word
what a time!

To me
that word says
it all.

Get away from
everyday life.
Escape
to another existence.

Perhaps
moving from
far left
to extreme right.

Well!
I have a two-fold
dream.

It is to see the sun,
rise on some
eastern coast,

and to see the sunset
on some
western shore.

In 2000, the first happened
in Fort Lauderdale, Florida
as I attended a national convention.

It was amazing,
our hotel room faced the east.

What a glorious site
to awaken with
God's brilliant sun

shinning forth
as it has done
since creation.
What a sight!

At this time
I'm waiting
for the second half

to come into existence.
Yes,
I'm still dreaming.

Beatrice Anderson (Miss Bea)

TEXAS CITY 1999

A good day
to remember,
watching people pass by,
warming under a pleasant sun,
blaring loudness, a stereo breaks
the silence, jarring the sidewalk,
but I don't care,
it's a great day to be young.

A brisk walk to the strip mall,
eating Chinese and rubbing Buddha's belly
four times for good luck,
salt fresh air awakening the senses,
began writing, listening
to sea gulls swooping
overhead, making their cries
sound important.

Antoinette V. Franklin

Fortune cookie says,
"You are master of every situation."

Reprinted with permission of Abide in the Spirit of Change 2012

"HAYWARD'S THOUGHTS ON HUMOR"

Humor is so good for our very soul,
Humor hides wrinkles that make us look old.
... puts a smile on a frowning face.
... brings about love where there is hate.

Humor can be a cure when you are feeling down.
... can come from just clowning around.
... can be antidote when feeling despair.
... is a way to show others we do care.

Humor will make you laugh instead of cry.
... replaces tears when we say goodbye.
... can come with a blink of an eye.
... allows us to tell a little white lie.

Humor aided us in becoming a great nation.
... livens up a party or any celebration.
... has been used by many famous speakers.
... is printed on clothes, shoes, even sneakers.

Humor when you think about what it has done.
... opens doors and makes life so much fun.
... can make you sick and healthy too,
... is an expression of everything we say or do.

Hayward Bethel (Guest Poet)

Reprinted with permission of Abide In the Spirit of Change 2012

MY GRANDMA ANNA CHAMBERS

A Poetic Picture of a Beautiful Lady

A little gray haired, wonderful, spirit filled lady
She was full of humor and wit.
Never an evil word did I hear her speak.
She loved to rock in her rocker, sing and sit.

I served as her chauffeur, and all around helper,
but I enjoyed every single minute she was awake,
for at 2 p. m. every day except Sunday you could rest assured
that she would stop for an afternoon nap she would take.

She used to teach me little colloquialism
and sing me songs of laughter and some of woe.
You could bet that if one listened close enough
The words would stick no matter where you go.

In every song there was a message to be heard
that dealt with life and most of them added a smile.
I believe there was a truism in each one of them
and they all have made my life worthwhile.

She taught Sunday School and loved singing hymns
and served as a Missionary and a Teacher.
She loved to work in the little church
as well as cook Sunday dinner for the preacher.

Many little songs she taught I could share with you,
but the one that always comes to mind
is the one that she would constantly sing,
that everything will always work out just fine.

The little song is called, "Smile N Grin,"
and I still sing it just about everyday.
I sing it out loud in the shower,
or whenever I need to brighten my way.

It brings me back to reality
for the joy to me it brings.
The words are very simple.
You too can learn it just listen while I sing.

Hayward Bethel

SMILE AND GRIN

A Song

Oh! It isn't any trouble than to smile (repeat twice)
It isn't any trouble than to S M I L E,
so smile when you're in trouble,
it will vanish like a bubble,
it isn't any trouble than to S M I L E.

Oh! It isn't any trouble than to grin (repeat twice)
It isn't any trouble than it will vanish like a bubble, to grin,
so G R I N when you're in trouble,
it will vanish like a bubble,
if you'll only take the trouble just to G R I N.
*(End of song)

Yes I do believe in yesterday
for all my troubles seem so far away,
for I can still hear my grandmother's voice,
her memories in my heart they will forever stay.

Laughter Heals, Smiles Soothe, and Grins grip

Hayward Bethel (Guest Poet)

Reprinted with permission from Abide in the Spirit of Change 2012

I wonder
at what stage
the scars and fears
of the past
will stop
catching us
by the throat
making us
afraid that around the
corner there is still someone
who will do us in--

I wonder
if the horrors
of the past
have given us
the strength
to fight back
both individually
and collectively

or if it has turned us
into people
who are more subdued
than before
by the powers around us.

When do we
teach each other
about the past as
a way to empower
rather than to
further suppress--

When do we stop
doing ourselves in?

George Bussey

FOR THE FAITHFUL AMONG US

The need for the past

is so much at the center of my life
I write this poem to record my discovery of it,
my reconciliation.
-Frank Bidart

I.
What is this sick attraction of mine,
this hissing beetle always in my ear,
reminding me of things left uncovered?

The city block I grew up on, for instance
was just a row of houses with terracotta roofs
of melting wax at dusk, when the sky was
haughty amber, and the day just ending
sped into the future like a shaking Amtrak car.

We were children, and thoughtless, pirates
and thieves, magical creatures, astronauts.
Whatever we could conjure with a box
upturned, and my grandfather's felt fedora;

I pretended to be a banker once, and wrote
"$100" on 50 index cards before noon
rolled us up in its humid dough, gingerbread
children stuck with our noses pointed down
at the hear-and-now, all because of Nick Nikola
told me

Jews have all the money

and I believed him.

II.

Hebrew school was just what we did every Sunday in the library of
temple Beth Jacob when I was 13.

And then we went to the Holocaust museum,

and I found a picture of Jewish woman
being burned.
And later a list of books by Helen Keller.

being burned.
And I asked Jacob Noakes' mother for the Hebrew word for
'fire'
but she didn't have it to give, so she gave me a
granola bar

and looked away.

III.

Now, I'll tell you something

secret:

I dreamed my share of dirty dreams

because I was a jealous Jew-child

in a classroom of gentiles,

trying my best to cut a blue star from a Christmas tree pattern.

I dreamed of Anne Frank asleep

with one eye open.

I dreamed of SS men shoveling bone-flakes settled in ash.

I fantasized about my classmates

                    bringing me pencils.

                and their leftover dinners

while I hid in the squalor of martyrdom

building this same jagged star of craft paper.

Deboughed pines laid one,

                  then other.

IV.

My first winter on my own was balmy.
The clouds filtered the sun's coronation, yellow
into a sweet wheat, and so I missed Chanukah
the way we miss idols

           we learn have died.

And the second year it crept up like a spider
from under a browning floorboard in the attic.

I used a potato as a menorah;
Nine white candles in nine sallow eyes.

I said the shehecheyanu in secret.

V.

September 1ˢᵗ, 1941. Berlin, Germany.

Dear Jew,

We have a challenge for the faithful among you:
Gather your altar, your silver graces.

Place every talisman you have
inside a cigar box. You'll find
there is no room for the scriptures,
the blessings, so you'll hold them in
your throat or just under your face,
between dreaming and action.

The rest will be embodied by a colored star.

VI.

What does a padlock's clicking sound like
in the memory? Does it draw you to the window
one bleak night, or stand you on your toes?

You'd pack a bag, grabbing what you could,
onions, apples. A shaving razor and a white jacket
emblazoned with the word 'mine.'

Quick, Count the silver! The tong of the forks, too.
Are there still four? Everything was taken from you, once.
What if it happened again?

Aaron Deutsch

WORDS

You ask for the concreteness of words
but I can't formulate my thoughts
a translucent wall of feeling
filters out the firm hardness of
labels and all I can provide is
the consequence of life lived

and that's the difference

through words
they have conquered
and enslaved our thoughts
until I don't know what is
breeding
and what is culture

Characterized, identified
they can name it
I cannot
all I have is the feeling dreamt
the empathy cried
and experience lived
a fountain of knowledge
shared

I can't decipher if it's
genuine infallibility,
the inside track, or the nitty-gritty
sometimes these naked truths
choke our poetic tongues
becloud our vision
and
shackle our hands to the ordinary

Denia Alvarado

I
EXPERIENCE

what differentiates this man from that one?
What turn of events:
what bit of luck;
what extension of a hand or lack thereof
created the man I see before me?

I've seen beauty wasted
minds altered by consequence
creativity shattered
and souls lost within humanity

the day laborer
holds a paint brush with his right hand
and a bucket of dreams with his left
the educated man
it seems
has no time to dream

II
HOPE

The water fountain
silent, not in neglect but in solitude
re energizes in summer blooms
that slowly turn golden
in autumn's call

Sleeping through the coolness of December
dreaming of children that learned to touch the gentle
stream of water
the water fountain
silent, not neglected, not forgotten,
re energizes for the awakening that is sure to come in

Spring

Denia Alvarado

A VERY HUMAN BEING

(Dedicated to the work of Imam W. Deen Mohammed)

I gave him just a passing glance-
His face and hair, his shirt and pants-
All covered in a split-second, no more;
After all, I'd seen "his kind" before...,

...But a spark in his eyes surprised me, and
He opened his mouth, and surprised me again
For what came from him came to me unexpected;
Its echo, inside me could not be rejected.

Experience deserted me, inside my brain went cold
Faced with a category that I couldn't pigeonhole;
"This one's not like the rest of them," but even I was seeing
My stereotypes refused to bend- to fit a human being!

I started getting angry then, but really at myself;
My noble lofty principles had fallen off their shelf
I had to reassess them, now confronted and adjusted.
For here- inside of my own mind- a bigot had been busted!

Life on the other worlds may seem impossible to find,
But here on earth, to recognize a human heart and mind
Is harder still for those who think that just a certain kind
Of people qualify, with all the rest somewhere behind!

The sorry truth is this for those who claim to have priority:
Denying others' birthright bares their own inferiority!
To change this sorry state of mind, disguised as "the human condition"
And remake the world, and remake ourselves,
Is every single human being's mission!

Imam Abdur-Rahim Muhammad of Auburn, New York

TO ALL MY BLACK BRETHREN

To all my Black brethren, whose history
has been to us- and others- a mystery
It's important to gain what we all used to lack,
but not to get all caught up in, "Basking in Black..."
just basking! Not even asking,
"Can I do what they did?"

Why Not!?!
They were once just a youth, child or kid!
They had obstacles, too trials worse! Or as bad...
But they also had something we don't seen to have had:
A Vision, A Purpose, and
Love for their Brother!
-enough at last, not to be killing each other!
Whether quickly or slowly, for no one relative gain
buy a modern-day enemy:
Live Body/Dead Brain!

Let our knowledge of history bring a new mind to life
for each son and daughter, every husband and wife:
So the whole world can see us grow proud of ourselves
and carve out of the present, a future that tells
just how we overcame, how we changed, how we grew-
so generations yet born, will feel proud of me and you!

(hajji) Abdur-Rahim Muhammad

TO BE A MAN

To be a Man: To see with Eyes

       Unclouded by self-centered Lies;

To be a Man : to be one Who

       Rejects the False, Accepts What's True;

To be a Man: One who can Measure

       Intelligence, growth against savage Pleasure;

To be a Man, No longer a Boy:

       Now one who can Build, Not one to destroy;

To be a Man: To face the great Test

       That Life gives to Those Who'd give it their Best!

To be a Man, Nevermore a Slave:

       Free ! To serve G'd:

              Free from Fear of the Grave!!!...

       ...No, I'm not yet a Man:

Still a Boy, like many of you.

       But, little boys have duties, too-

       So I'm working and trying,

       Hard as This Little Boy can

To be a Man,

To be a Man

To be a Man

a MAN!

(hajji) 'Abdur-Rahim Muhammad

✦

To be a Man,

To be a Man

To be a Man

a MAN!

(hajji) 'Abdur-Rahim Muhammad

AT "ELMER'S IT BE BAD!"

I took my date out one evening
to T-Town's "Elmer's It Be Bad!"
'Twas the best dine-in dating experience I ever had.
I never saw the young waitress
who took our orders and served.
My date had smooth skin and long, curly hair
as well as body with many curves.
My date was so good to look at
as were the ribs, brisket, and chicken.
Her lips were luscious looking
as I watch them sucking them bones,
smacking and licking.
This dining experience made me glad.
'Twas some serious communion between us at
"Elmer's It Be Bad!"
I was sweating down there
at "Elmer's It Bed Bad!"
Tasted the best fire-hot Route 66
country barbeque sauce I ever had.
I liked this woman as much
as I liked that good food.
For the money I paid,
it was a delicious deal.
Watching her enjoy that soul food
was an especially satisfying thrill;
the way she ate that food with her fingers,
making pleasing sounds that were not at all bad;
the way she was impressively dressed for leisure,
looking inviting and loosely clad.
As a gentleman, I treated her politely
but inside I screamed, "Ooh Mama! You So Hot!! E-gad!!!"
That evening, we were one greasy mouthed couple
at "Elmer's: It Be Bad!"

A E. Doyle

WHAT I REMEMBER ON OUR WEDDING DAY

I remember that beam of joy on your face,
I remember that glow and radiant smile,
I remember you like an angel of sunshine
as you walked down the wedding aisle.

I remember how nervous we both were
as you stood to the left of me.
My heart was beating hard and fast
during that entire ceremony.

I remember when we exchanged our vows.
I remember when I slipped the ring on your finger.
Our wedding song was the hit of the seventies hit song "Inseparable".
The choir lady who sang it was a fabulous singer.

I remember when we kissed and I dipped you at the altar.
I remember the Pastor pronouncing us man and wife.
Then we looked deeply into each others eyes
and vowed we would stay together for life.

I remember the reception and the well wishers.
Then there was the wedding night.
Now, that was a memory I could never forget;
you were indescribable. My, oh my, what a sight!

You were a portrait of beauty that day
as you have always been.
I shall love you forever!
As my bride, my wife, and my best friend.

A. E. Doyle

CHAOS ON THE BUS

You should have been seen it, a few country flies
in a moving air conditioned express city bus.
They were flying around and around,
landing on and irritating us.

You could sense the ire of the passengers.
On their faces, you could see the disgust.
Then suddenly, somebody went "Three Stooges".
It was hit, be hit, or get off the bus.

Father Mulligan was poked in the eye.
He had to lean over to adjust.
An old lady was slapped on her head.
In reaction, she screamed and she fussed.

A young rapper was punched in the jaw.
He rhymed and rhythmically rapped as he cussed.
An off-duty cop was slapped in his face.
"He reacted but Miranda rights were not read are discussed."

Another guy was belted in the belly.
He bent over because his lunch came up.
A hood rat was slapped on his ear.
He rose up and threatened to kick somebody's butt.

A large lady swung her massive plus-sized arm
when she was kicked in her gut.
There was such utter chaos, confusion and turmoil.
It is as if some spirit invaded to seize us.

A librarian with ham-hocked ashy ankles called for order.
There was no civility, unity and trust.
This ghetto sista's wig was knocked off.
She reached in to pull out a switchblade
from inside her big bosomy bust.

It happened on a reduced ozone alert day
as the bus moved through road construction dust.
The bus driver, listening to music through his MP3 earplugs,
never heard the melee on his bus.

The scene inside that bus was so surreal.
It was at that moment that I looked up.
I saw those flies perched on the ceiling,
Transfixed on people's drama and looking down at all of us

A. E. Doyle

"Do Right"

S. J. Sutton
one of the first principle of Phyllis Wheatley High School
1934-1939
San Antonio, Texas

"Once you have learned to read
you will be forever free."

Frederick Douglas
former slave, abolitionist

SHORT STORIES
PART II

"A CHANGE IS GONNA COME"

"Darkness cannot drive out darkness; only light can do that.
Hate cannot drive hate; only Love can do that."

Dr. Martin Luther King Civil Right Leader

STARS

Photo by Rafael F.

THE ASCENT OF DOVES

Antoinette V. Franklin

A tall well-dressed man spoke in a monotone as the remaining mourners began to leave the cemetery. He said, "Good sister Rosemary Clark was a dedicated church worker and always gave freely to Sainted Heaven, her church home for over twenty-five years. She gave more than necessary and would do so without being asked. The church and community will deeply miss her kind words and warm smile. The church has prepared luncheon and you may now be dismissed.

Mrs. Dawson spoke first as the chirp of the car alarm sounded. "My, did you ever hear such foolishness? Why, I have never seen such. That funeral was way too long. They treated her as if she was a dignitary and if that wasn't bad enough now they have Lewis playing a violin in the cemetery. Lord child today she replied."

Mrs. Cline stifled a giggle as she adjusted her seat belt. "Yeah, undertaker Jones was talking about how she gave her money without being asked. She would have the exact amount announced every Sunday in church. Everyone knew that "ole lady Clark" had told the church secretary to make that announcement because she felt if the people knew how much she gave, then they would be inspired to give more. She would sit back and gloat when the amount was given. You know giving is a personal thing and you know some folks couldn't give much. The good book talks about "(The Widows Mite.)"

"Yeah, she was always ready to point out someone's short comings," added Mrs. Dawson. She would tell folk she always had her mind stayed on the good Lord and his mighty word. She had her mind on everybody else's business," added Mrs. Cline.

Mrs. Dawson merged with oncoming traffic and said, "I was truly grateful when she stopped trying to cook and started giving money instead." "If that ain't the truth," laughed Mrs. Cline added, "Now, Irene you know Rosemary couldn't boil water on a good day, not at all. You remember that extra yellow brick of pound cake she brought to the church festival. The cake was the last remaining dessert on the table.

It was so heavy the card table sagged in the center from the weight and we could never figure why it was so yellow. Reverend Simpson felt sorry for her and paid five dollars for that thing. He didn't want her feelings to be hurt. "I heard that Mrs. Simpson made him put in it trash. She didn't want that awful looking thing in her house. I bet those disposal workers had a time lifting the receptacle Monday morning." The two women chuckled with delight.

"Now Agnes," began Mrs. Dawson, "It is not nice to speak ill of the dead, but remember that barbecue dinner with those burned pinto beans and the little bitty chicken legs. Rosemary had bragged about how good her beans were, they'd melt in your mouth, was her boast, but she got upset when Deacon Smith asked for a refund."

She told him, "That he was donating to the church and for him to get over himself and she didn't refund his six dollars and fifty cents either." He told her told that nobody wanted to eat burnt food and those chicken legs, must have been stolen from a baby bird. But she still wouldn't give him the money back.

The two women continued down the highway when Mrs. Cline spoke saying, "Rosemary Clark was a sight and when she donated, she made sure that she would be reimbursed. That woman could make an eagle squeak when it came to her money."

The poor people of Sainted Heaven avoided her. I would count my words whenever I had to speak with her. If she didn't know your business she would surely embellish it. Mrs. Dawson nodded in agreement and added, "Ole Lady Clark was quite a snoop, spiteful and was mean tempered."

"I heard that she was run out of two churches before settling at Sainted Heaven." replied Mrs. Cline. Mrs. Dawson added, "Yeah, I bet it was because of her wagging tongue. She had been married four times and that husband before Mr. Clark, died of an unexplained illness. Many people still believe she poisoned Mr. Clark." The deacons were so sympathetic for Mr. Clark, the poor man.

My Leroy used to say, "Dying was the first peace poor Herman ever had, living with that woman, many of the men were glad their wives were not like her."

Mrs. Dawson shook her head and asked, "Remember that incident last year at the Christmas Brunch? Mrs. Cline responded, "Who could forget?" Mrs. Dawson began, "Everyone knew bad blood and unkind words had been spoken between Mrs. Clark and Mrs. Rudolph before."

Lizzie Rudolph had told Mrs. Clark at the church picnic, "She was going to slap all those rat titties from off her head if she didn't stop messing with her family". "You know those two were a pair cut from the same cloth, always trying to out do each other."

Mrs. Dawson continued, Mrs. Clark made a comment when Mrs. Rudolph introduced Ruby's new husband. She said in a loud whisper, "She didn't marry anything," (not realizing or caring that Mrs. Rudolph was in earshot.)

Mrs. Rudolph jerked her head around so fast she almost lost her balance. Her words slapped the pine sent off of the Christmas tree and the music skipped a beat as she replied "Don't you be talking about my son-in-law. At least Isaac is a good God-fearing man with a good job. Your daughter should be so lucky. She's forever borrowing some woman's husband and doesn't know who her children's daddies are. She's down right shameful, forever draping herself around somebody's man like second skin and being proud of it.

The church group held their breath as the two women glared at each other like brooding hens. If the reverend hadn't spoken up it would have been a knock down, drag out brawl with those two uncouth women.

Mrs. Clark squared her shoulders and narrowed her dark eyes and straightened her feather, sequined hat, then waddled out of the reception hall to the relief of everyone. Poor Mr. Clark went trailing quickly behind her; begging everyone's pardon as he exited.

That woman was a piece of work, always using five-dollar words with her fifty-cent brain. It was a shame she was so illiterate, all pretense and Tom Foolery, couldn't read, write or follow directions. She would sit and brag about Mr. Clark having a degree from Bishop College yet wouldn't attend a classes to help herself.

She surely had the reverend fooled or it might have been the fifty dollar bills she glazed across his palm. Mrs. Cline asked, "Do you remember that god awful desk she bought for his anniversary? That monstrosity of oak couldn't fit through the doors. They had to remove the hinges and then it was stuffed in that small office. They both began to chuckle until Mrs. Cline snorted and said, "You are gonna make me wet myself."

After she bought that ugly thing she then declared herself mother of the church and position for women is selected not self appointed. That day she wore a new feathered, flowered concoction and a long evening gown for that announcement. Mrs. Simpson and the other women were totally shocked, she nearly fainted.

This whole event has been something else. When I walked into Peaceful Care Funeral Parlor I had to compose myself. She was laid out in that too little white casket with an oversized white orchid, a gold evening gown with elbow length white gloves and a golden tam cocked on her head. I tell you I almost lost it. Girl she looked like a big black bear in that white casket. Why undertaker Jones should have been ashamed of himself.

Well you know those were her wishes replied Mrs. Dawson. It's not his fault Dinah wouldn't pay for a larger casket to fit her over sized mother into. What really took the cake was the scene at the cemetery. Mrs. Clark had left instructions to have three dozen white doves released as her body was placed into the bosom of the earth. These doves would signify that she had made her ascent into heaven. As the crane lowered the coffin, Alfred played the violin. He was dressed in a black tux with tails. His father read a poem about the ascent of doves meaning the soul of the deceased raising to meet the angels and being taken to the Father.

The doves were trained to circle twice and return on command, but these doves didn't get the message they never got off the ground. Mr. Jones then instructed his staff to run towards the doves in order to get them airborne, but the creatures gently parted as the staff approached. As Mrs. Dawson pulled to a stop and said, "Those dove feathers never took flight," they're still pecking at the bare ground.

*This story was entered into the Writers Digest Sort Story Contest February 2012. I have added it so others could read the story. Whenever I have work that isn't accepted I publish the writing myself.

...WHEN I WAS COLORED

Linda Ruth Sheppard Oliver

My name is Linda Ruth Sheppard Oliver. I was born in 1951 in Gordon, Arkansas, about two o'clock in the morning. This was a time when colored babies couldn't be born in white hospitals, a time of "Separate but Not Equal," a time just before Brown vs. the Board of Education. Colored babies had to be delivered by midwives. It was the midwife who helped you connect to the Creator, through the birth of life.

My mother, who was not from Arkansas but knew the unspoken rules, became uncontrollable when the labor pains came. She rushed to the white clinic, knowing that was a major no-no, but what can you say to a desperate woman who is about to give birth shouting, "Let me in, Let me in now." Miss Alma, the midwife, was off delivering another colored baby reaching for breath. So my mother went to a white clinic to make her presence known.

There was Ruth, crying and trying to keep silent during the pain that brings forth life. The staff was moving around her in the room as if she was a stolen piece of property. Not knowing that she was the thief; stealing the towels, water, medicine, instruments and the skills of the doctor and nurses who were helping her birth her baby.

Before you knew it, I was here 8 lbs and 8 oz., a big baby. Those hands that would not allow me in the doors, but allowed me in their arms held me. Me with no hair and I was not the color you would expect a colored baby. You know the brown fingertips, or the markings on the ears. In fact, I couldn't even pass for Colored. But looking at my mother, they all knew I was Colored.

All of my past inheritance was given to me without my even knowing it. Yes, the Native American, the Slave, the Spaniard, the Colored Man and the Colored Woman. The two sets of Robinson, the dark side and the light side, all showed up in me without warning. My lineage from three continents: Africa, Europe, and the Americas, each of them in the room when I showed up.

That is what happened to me in my Colored Ville, I didn't understand there were other ethnicities within my own family. All these love affairs were present and I never knew it until I was over forty. The secret had held itself until I saw my family's faces of other Native Americans, Spaniards, and Mexicans. I saw my Grandpa's face on other people who looked just like him. All I ever knew was that they were just, "Grandpa" and "Mother Doll" and "Mother Dear" and "Uncle Big Man," not Black or White or Mexican nor Native American or Colored!

I was born without papers, no birth certificate, nothing. It wasn't until I was on my way to college that I discovered that I was without papers to show that I was American. So, I got creative. I, Linda Ruth, had to create my own birth record with the facts being allowed to move in and out of truths. I worked very hard to not put Elvis's name in the line that was designed for my father. It wasn't easy!

My mother worked in a white family's home, so I didn't know that there wasn't a difference between them and me. I was attending school at Holy Cross and the nuns treated me with so much love that I didn't even see color. I was a child of God with hope of becoming a nun, yes, me, I wanted to be a nun. Not because of the call to God on my life, but because they had great peanut butter and jelly sandwiches. I went to the third grade, that's where it all began when we moved to San Antonio from Corpus Christi; new schools, new home, new friends and new colored people.

The first time I was called a "Nigger" I was nine years old, the same year I had the greatest Christmas ever. That was the year I received everything I ever wanted. I got the doll, the bicycle, the doctor and nurse kit and tons of cookies and candy filling my stocking to the brim. This was the same year I was called a "Nigger."

I remember running home to my mother and asking, "Momma what's a "Nigger?" As I look back now, I still don't know how she really answered that one. A "Nigger" at nine! The double "N." Truth be told, the child that uttered that word to me, her face was darker than mine.

I guess that was the beginning of self-hatred. Both of us trapped in skins that knew no better. Name-calling and fighting were the two most embedded behaviors that Coloreds knew. I once thought that playing "The Dozens" was the way to ensure that you would not become a junkie, a drunk, a slut or a whore. Name-calling, allowed you to get the pain out without showing your true self. It was a guarantee that you would be safe from it all. Thank God we didn't know we were building bridges to hate, fear and pain.

Of course there were choices, and yes I chose fighting. It was fighting that kept me safe. Safe from others who were bigger than me, smarter than me and slower than me. Fighting was the way to go. Fighting was my outlet. It called my name, for so many years. I was caught in the web of her might, without knowing that it only meant that I was unable to stop the pain, the fear and the hurt.

I was in love with fighting. I fact, I saw people giving a..-kicking to each other like gifts. Hitting each other with ugly words and phrases, cutting into love with ugly digs that went beyond love and found their place in silence. I fought in school, I fought at home and I fought at the playground. I fought to get ahead and I fought to become.

The Bible taught that fighting was righteous, from Moses fighting the Egyptians; to David fighting Goliath, the giant. Fighting became Godly and Holy. Yes I was one of those girls that fought everyday! In fact I would fight by appointments. You know, I would come to your house, knock on the door and ask if you were ready for your a.. kicking. I would give you time to reconsider the whole ordeal.

I always gave them a few minutes to think it over. I was so bold to ask my opponents, to please bring their lunch and to invite their family members, because they were more than welcome to get their a.. kicked as well. It was a family thing in my mind.

Then one day, I had become a B....!!! Yea!!! All of that fighting placed me in the role of having to fight for all of my yes's and no's in my own mind, I was the little colored girl who loved to fight and that made me crazy. I feared no one, and no thing! OK, I lied, there were some things I was afraid of the mummies and the monsters that played on the screen every weekend. Running across those tracks to get home was no joke and if the moon was full, I ran even harder, often leaving my brothers far behind. I was not afraid of the "real things," but the "not real things," now that's a different story. Too bad that my opponents couldn't have placed garlic around their necks, to keep Linda Ruth away from attacking them, like I did to keep the Wolf Man and Dracula off of me.

I remember going into the Cameo Theater for movies; that place was the best! It allowed you to bring your own lunch. I always had peanut butter and jelly sandwiches on hand and there was no shame because the Cameo was not segregated like the Majestic. I remember the first time I was able to stroll in the front door and sit in row 1, seat 19 and hear Johnny Mathis, OOOH! He was wonderful!!!

Living in Colored Ville meant that you weren't allowed to shop in clothing stores, because you were forbidden to try clothes on. In fact, I thought everybody shopped with Mr. Salmon. He would come to your home and you would shop out of the trunk of his automobile. Actually, I was 21 years before I received my first coat bought for me that I tried on the store!

Now I realize why playing closet, (which means getting hand-me-downs) was such a blast! It was my way of shopping for years. I didn't see why I enjoyed it so much then, until I stopped and said, "Oh that is why I act like this," still wanting to shop outside in those flea markets.

Being Colored was the best when it came to having fun. The Black Soc Stadium on Saturdays would be filled with people from all over the city watching baseball. Men and women enjoyed the barbecue served and having the sun slide down over the horizon while witnessing children fall asleep in the arm of everyone.

Women wearing pretty hats and summer dresses that seemed to fit their tiny waists. The players giving their best and fighting to share their skills with each of us. As if we knew that one day we were going to be free enough to play in a space where everyone would be treated like humans, yes, humans. We had to work harder than everyone else and be smarter than everyone else, to keep the "Colored" from being seen. As if it would ooze out on your clothes and stain the place you were sitting.

That brings to mind the first time I was treated differently for being Colored, I was about 12 years old, while reading about Jesus doing his father's business, when I saw a sign reading "Colored only" in Bastrop, Texas. I guess it was around the early sixties, before JFK was killed. So strange that you can remember the very moment that you felt when the shots rang out. You can remember the clothes you had on and the class you were in, the tears running down your face, he's dead!

All of my hopes were gone. JFK and Martin Luther King molded me into someone who fought even harder, this time for my rights and my freedom, for the ideals of America. The America I heard I was a citizen of. The constitution, the law of the land, the home of the brave and the free, wasn't talking about me. America, the one that placed high honors on its children and it's citizens, but only if they were white! That America died in the sixties.

Oh, I'm getting away from the story, "Colored only" signs; my mother wanted us to go and eat at this restaurant where whites and Colored/Negros were able to eat under the same roof where there were tables and chairs for families to share their meals, "The World's Greatest Barbeque." We all walked to the counter, to order our food and the place went silent. All of the white people, and I do mean all of them stopped eating. The men, the women, and the children froze in mid-chew as we walked in They looked as if we just came from another planet! Like they never had seen a Colored person in their entire life, as if no colored person was looking after their children, or cleaning their homes. Yes, they looked at me as if I had just beamed down from a yellow and purple spaceship and I had to share their air! If looks could kill, we were dead! As dead as you get!

They watched us walk up to the counter and a huge white man asked, "How many?" My mother answered, "There are six of us." He strolled over to the counter and began to tear off sheets of butcher paper, one sheet for each of us, for plates. These sheets of butcher paper were to be our plates. We all stood there with no word coming from our mouths. I don't recall if we huddled together, as if the ball game was about to start, or if we just stood there, each of us in our own silence. It was the longest moment I had ever lived through. The words that often came out of my mouth when I was fighting lay still in my being. I had an extensive vocabulary of cuss words crowded in my being with nowhere to go, not even in my mind. I was waiting, but my words just couldn't come.

My mother, the proud woman, who had washed these people's clothes, cleaned their homes and had taken care of their children. My mother who had listened to Mr. Elliot when things were not going well at work, and to Miss Elliot when she didn't understand why her life was so filled with untruths. My mother was waiting for words to come. It appeared as if they were lost, and then all of a sudden, out of the depths of her being came these words, "Oh no, we won't be eating it here, we'll be taking it home." The man acted as if he had gotten lost in her directions from the beginning, looked stunned. I was so proud of her. She stood up to the man, the laws, the constitution, the stories, the doubt and what might happen next!

All the shame that she had worked to shield me from was standing in the middle of it all, Colored/White/Hate/Fear! Now I was Colored, and being treated like I was Colored. At that point, I woke up to the word that I had heard three years earlier, the big "N" word was out! This time I felt the word and my mother didn't have to share that meaning with me ever again.

That day I was Colored and knew it.

JUST SEND ME A BILL

Patricia Schwindt

Targovshte, Bulgaria
November 1992

No one told me any differently, so I was surprised one day to find my phone dead. With hands and feet, I asked the lady at the desk in my building, we call The Post Office, and then told me with her hands and feet and a gesture known internationally to mean pay, that I had to pay the bill.

Bill? What bill? I never got one. I told Polina, the Russian woman who teaches English with me at my school. You won't get one, she said. *You go to the Post Office* once a month and, tell them your number and pay whatever they tell you.

Okay, no bill, no receipt and no record of the calls I made. Well, thanks for telling me, I muttered on the way to the post office the next morning.

So now I'm standing in line again. I hate standing in these eternal lines here. Everywhere I go, I have to stand in line. Want some flour and a leaky plastic bottle of weak bleach at the grocery store? Stand in line. Want some bread at that little hut down the street? Stand in line. Want to look at that pair of boots back behind the counter in that little tin shack with "Shop" on the sign outside? You guessed it. Stand in line and wait for the clerk to talk to you. If she's not doing a crossword puzzle or filing her nails, that is.

You really can't blame her. That's how it worked all the years since she got her first job. The market in communist countries was not customer-oriented; shops, restaurants and other businesses got paid the same, whether they sold anything or not. If you didn't like your food, or if was cold when it came to you, tough luck. If you couldn't get the fabric you needed to make a dress, tough luck. Whenever you went as a customer, whatever you wanted, it was usually the same story. Take it or leave it. If there was anything to take.

Americans don't like this philosophy, and I am no exception. About the time I'm ready to incite a riot among the other weary people standing in line with me, I finally make it to the front. At this precise moment, the clock ticks forward to 10:00 and the lady on the other side slams the window shut.

What? Hey, I have to go to work! Open up back there!

Putchiva, the people behind me say, as if it's no big deal. *Coffee break.*

Oh, no you don't. I think to myself. *Bull cookies on the coffee break when you've got twenty people standing here on tired feet.*

I rap on the window, shove a slip of paper at her with my phone number on it and wave money at her, repeating over and over in my best Bulgarian: *Me go to work. Az rabot! Az rabot!*

She rolls her eyes, shakes her head and takes my money.

I go to work.

From "Conquering the Stand-up Toilet: and other stories about living and teaching in Bulgaria".

MAKING FRIENDS WITH THE WASHING MACHINE

Patricia Schwindt

Targovishte, Bulgaria
September 1992

First, the good news. I came home one afternoon to find that my promised washing machine had been delivered. Now, the bad news.

This thing looks nothing like any vision I've ever had of a washing machine. It is about two feet square and a foot and a half tall. Made of blue and white plastic, it has two hoses tucked inside the plastic rotating drum under the lid on the top. It weighs about 12 pounds. I'd guess. Now, the worse news. An instruction booklet accompanying the machine first offered me some hope, then it dashed it all. The instructions were written in Russian.

Two weeks later, after no success in finding someone with the time to come and show me how it works, I'm determined to tackle it myself. I have the day off from class, so I'll cook myself a fine breakfast of fried potatoes and onions. But only after I get my laundry going. First things first.

After thirty futile minutes with the Russian instructions in one hand and my very poor dictionary in the other, I put the useless paper aside and drag the machine out of the bathroom.

Turning it on its head, I examine all the ins and outs of the "machinery" housed at the back, and the two knobs on the top. The knob marked "Regime" must be 'cycle', I surmise, because the other knob, with an orange flame symbol beside it, has to be water temperature.

With that figured out, I pull out two hoses and wrestle another 30 minutes away, trying to persuade them to slide onto their respective spigots at the back: one to bring water from the sink in to the cabinet surrounding the plastic rotating drum, the other to drain it out. The drum looks like the surface of a cheese grater, so the water must flow through the holes to the clothes inside the drum. If I can get these attached to this thing, that is!

Finally, I turn a table knife into a rubber-stretcher and insist that the hose couple up with the connection. First the hose to drain the water out, and then the one to bring the water in. Voila! Who needs instructions??

Now I roll the machine a few feet then pick it up and carry it to the cement-floored cubicle that passes as a shower, where I attach the bulbous end of the "in" hose to the top on my shower faucet. The other hose I tuck into the drainpipe hole in the floor. This floor is made of coarse, grey-flecked concrete and I have long since stopped worrying about the water as it splashes everywhere in this "shower room". It's supposed to do that. With both in place, I survey my success to this point, quite satisfied.

Now what? Okay, I know when to ask for expert help, so I trip lightly down the stairs to Apartment 1, where a friendly staff woman is always on duty. How hard can it be for her to show me what to do next? *Come with me,* I ask with hands and feet, *Pet...na...decet...minooti* I have learned to say in Bulgarian. *Fifteen minutes.* She comes, and I show Maria what I need.

She fiddles with it awhile, checks the hoses and looks puzzled, but then she turns the water on and smiles, motioning for me to put the dirty clothes in. *Pet kilogram*, she says, Good. I can get five kilos of laundry in there, so I load in my underwear, towels and dish towels.

I soon learn, incidentally, that 12 pounds is about ten pounds too much for that little drum, and over time I perfected a system for washing small batches with the same sudsy water before draining it out, and then starting over with fresh water to rinse everything. Doing the laundry wound up being a major chore, as it took all day to get it done this way. But I never complained. Most women, I discovered, had no machine at all and did their family's laundry by hand.

We sprinkle a plastic juice cup full of cheap Russian laundry soap over the clothes, and smugly snap the lid shut on the rotating drum. With great fanfare, Maria turns the dial. Nothing. She fiddles with another knob, still nothing.

Aha! She picks up the cord and plugs it into the socket, and the machine starts humming and tumbling as the water trickles in.

Maria beams with satisfaction on her way out, and as it's noon by now, I head for the kitchen to cook my potatoes and onions. When I've finished,

I noticed that the machine has stopped. *Great*, I think, expecting to find my clothes rinsed and spun and ready to hang out on the balcony.

Wrong. The tub is still full of soapy water, although the dial has made its round and is again on "off". I'll run it through again, I mutter, and start the thing over again. *This time, the new water coming in will rinse away the old, the sudsy.*

Wrong again. All that does is flood water into the compartment housing the motor, and that makes me pretty nervous. An hour later, three more cycles, I give up, wring the clothes out by hand, then pick up the machine, turn it on its head again, and drain it myself.

I wonder if the Maytag Man makes house calls to Bulgaria.

From "Conquering the Stand-up Toilet: and other stories about living and teaching in Bulgaria". By Patricia Collins Schwindt

LESSONS

...after abuse,
torment and unhappiness,
I learned I am beautiful,
talented, giving, loving,
forgiving and a spiritual being.
I have survived.

Antoinette V. Franklin

Reprinted with permission of Poets Along the River 1999

BLUE

Linda Ruth Sheppard Oliver

He came into the room when the lights were no longer on, where the lights glowed from another source, maybe it was the kitchen or the bathroom light. Mama left, one light on for sleepwalking, when we had to go to the bathroom, when she wanted to keep the sheets dry and clean.

Like a giant cat moving about without a sound, he was in our house. I don't know if he passed by the room where she slept and had seen everything was clear, or just moved into our room to make his hit and then move on.

I had just been talking to God hours earlier, me and Winston were on our knees saying, "Now I lay me down to sleep, I pray the Lord my soul to keep, if I should die before I wake, I pray the Lord my soul to take." God bless; Mommy, Daddy, Grand Maw, Grand Paw, Uncle Leon, Uncle Scottie, Aunt Alma, Aunt Rainlola.

Winston stopped giving up names while I continued with all of my cousins and there were 35 of them, God bless the neighbors, the dogs and cats. I would include everybody so I could stay up longer past my bedtime.

Then he came, the blue uniform slipped in without a warning, as if he was given an invitation from the family of madness. The family of madness had taken many of our men. The men at the barber shop talked about how Freddie's sister was his momma. His father was going to the penitentiary for a long time because he had caused his step momma, his wife so much pain, now she's taking care of them both, the sister, momma, as well as little Freddie and her own child too.

Freddie's momma/sister never learned to love Freddie, because she couldn't understand the family madness and she became mad. The family of madness lived too close to our homes sometimes, they spoke to us and watched us play. Sometimes they came over for dinner, sang songs from the radio and they even shared last names.

But what does it mean, when the family of madness comes to grab their daughters. The men from the family of madness were given the okay to sleep on top of children. They thought that it was okay to lay with girls and boys, who knew no voice.

These men who want you from afar, who offer candy, because they know that would allow you to follow. The men who manage to fondle you because you don't know how your body should respond to his hand as it brushes across your flowered shirt.

They put you on their laps in order to get a rise out of their pants. Placing their hands in places that aren't understood by children. They used drink to share their victories and tell their stories as if it was a welcome notes of a lost horn.

My mother hadn't talked about the way my body would change, or that one day it would look different no longer bald, nothing about the birds and the bees, nor the ways in which the family of madness would hurt little girls and little boys when we were innocent.

Now the silence that was on me; the man in the blue pushing my hands away from my panties, trying not to wake me up as if he didn't want me to see my eyes and my body not weighing 65 lbs. I was laying there with my hands between my legs, not wanting to lay on my back, forcing me to give away my innocence, without words. My body laid there as if trying to wake up from the deep, but I couldn't understand why his hand was on mine, or why he was trying to put his hands in me. I lay there and kept me sleeping not seeing the eyes of the man in blue, or the family of madness that was now laying beside me with his hands between my legs.

I had slipped into the deep sleep, but my hands knew that there had not been other hands that had placed themselves on my private. My hands knew that I was sleep, but they had to protect me from the man's hands in the blue.

He was beside me as if he was my cousins, Pam or Donnie; someone we had shared our bed with before. The man in blue never told the story about how he caught a cat and put him into a trash can and banged on the trash can with a stick, or how long it took him to wash dishes when we had duck for dinner that was our pet. Or how Jesus fed the children and the five thousand on the mount.

No, he didn't say a word, he and I hadn't shared stories, nor ice cream; all I ever knew was that he was on me and I didn't know how to wake up, nor did I know how to keep him from getting into my panties.

The men of the family of madness must have had special powers because the doors didn't protect me, the windows didn't protect me and my daddy didn't protect me and my mother may have been in the other room, but she couldn't protect me.

I couldn't say a word because me and sleep were rolled up as if sheets were on the line without the wind's laughter, nor the sun's warmth, or the clouds to tell your story that God wanted to share.

It was sleep, my hands and the prayers that now held me. Not the blue uniform man, not the day I had lost to life, not the eyes that were in my head, not the silence of my words, not to sighs in my heart, just God and my hands.

Tugging at my panties, he was trying to put his hands between my legs without saying a word or even trying to wake me up. My brother sleeping in the same bed was not bothering with him, because being in our bed with us is what we had learned to do, share because so many times we have had to share these sheets with all of the families that moved in and out of our home. We were sharing ourselves, our food, our stories, and even sharing our madness.

Sharing is what we knew, I tried to wake up, but that time of morning/night wouldn't allow my eyes to open. He kept placing his hands back, the sound of nothing was present in the room, just that blue uniform with no name.

I still didn't understand why he would crawl into our bed; the one that was safe for children, the place where we told and shared stories. Where we kept clean sheets on, the one we drew outlines of clouds on.

Our bed was for children, now trying to take my childhood away from me with his penis, trying to place it inside of me. Men who knew that one day that the child in me would have to have a voice; one day the man in blue would have to come to terms with the blues in me.

Over and over trying to get my hands to move the Tuesday panties that would not give.

My teacher told us girls, be careful about how you dress.
If you don't dress appropriately and a man looks at you with
"Lustful Eyes," it's like teasing a hungry dog with a juicy steak.

LaBertha Gibson
Home Economic Instructor
Blackshire High School
La Mesa, Texas

...WHILE STANDING IN LINE
AT THE HANDY ANDY

Antoinette V. Franklin

The line was unusually long at the neighborhood Handy Andy Grocery Store. I had come in for a few needed items and my pretty baby was sound asleep in her carrier in the basket. I finally arrived in front of the magazine counter and I reached for a magazine to help pass the time away.

I wasn't planning to buy the magazine because it didn't fit into my budget. I was buying the necessary items: two package of generic pampers, ten cans of formula, a few bananas, lady personal items and those necessary sanitary pads. Also in the basket was a small package of hamburger and one small whole fryer, some carrots and lettuce for a salad.

As I continued to read about fifty ways to please your man, I thought *"Where do they come up with this stuff?"* Someone has quite an imagination, but I kept reading, when I was interrupted by a lady putting her hand into the basket about to touch my baby. I have a problem with people touching me and was not thrilled about strangers touching my baby. I put the magazine down and stared at a cinnamon colored woman with a salt and pepper neatly styled Afro. She smiled as she withdrew her hand and said, "She sure is a pretty baby. Look at all of that hair. Is this your first?" My baby kept on sleeping peacefully as the lady continued.

I answered, "Thank-you and yes to the last question," still watching her. There had been a baby stolen from a basket in another city and my senses were being stretched to the limit. But the lady seemed harmless and I began to relax. The lady kept oohing and ah-hing and finally said, "She looks like you." I smiled slightly because some people had stated that she didn't.

The line was still not moving and I really didn't feel like talking. But the new clerk had asked for a price check, the cash register had ran out of paper and the other customers were becoming quite testy. So I took a deep breath and prepared to wait, but the lady began talking again while pulling out her wallet that unfolded unto the floor.

She introduced herself as Doris and showed me her three daughter's pictures. There was an assortment of colorful faces in various stages of growth, elementary, junior high and then high school.

These photos were of three pretty brown skinned girls with freckles and pony-tailed hairdos and some with full Afros. Miss Doris showed me one picture at a time and gave their names and little history about each one. She said, "This is Betty, she's a nurse, This is Roxanne, she's a teacher, and this is my baby Deidre, she's a legal secretary at a firm downtown.

The sight of my smile encouraged her to continue and I told her my name and my daughter's name. She told me how pretty both names were. Before I could add another word she told me how she had raised her children by herself, and had never been on welfare. She said, "She pushed a broom and mop that were bigger then she was, but held her head high because she had a job."

Miss Doris told me that her daughters never went without anything. She shared that her husband had ran off and left her when the girls were very young, but she had survived. She wanted me to keep praying and hold my head high and she finally asked if I had a job?

But before I could answer she said, "Don't let nobody make you feel less than what you are." I was stunned because those were the same words my father used to tell me when I was younger. It was as if my father was speaking through her.

Miss Doris looked sternly into my eyes and said "Honey you gonna do a fine job and be a good mother." She finally added everything is gonna be fine. I really wanted to cry because I was a single mother, struggling as hard as I could to make everything work out for me and Alexis, my daughter.

Miss Doris patted my hand and told me, "You keep being a good mother, take care of this pretty baby and don't think about no welfare." I gave her a shaky "OK." She shook her head in agreement and I placed the magazine back onto the shelf.

And placed my meager items on the counter, gave the clerk my twenty dollar bill and received my two dollars back. I always asked God to at least let me have two dollars to tide me over, at least I could buy gas until pay day. In the 1980's things were not quite as expensive, but it was still a struggle. I had a job, a used mustang and was buying a house for me and my baby. We were surviving.

I often think of Miss Doris and her story of taking pride in working hard taking care of her children and not being on welfare. Her words linger in my mind, "Work hard and don't get on welfare."

"People are dream killers. You've got to be careful
who you give emotional access to."

Tyree Gibson

TEMPEST

Karen McDonald (Tempest)

"How my life has been brought to undiscovered lands, and how much richer it gets-all from words printed...How a book can have 560 pages but in only three pages change the reader's life."

Emoke B'Raez Writing in Malaprop's Newsletter

ESSAYS
PART III

WORDS TO INSPIRE

"Any book that helps a child to form a habit of reading,
to make reading one of his deep and continuing needs is good for him."

Maya Angelou

BORED

Antoinette V. Franklin

My mother always said, "Idle hands is the devil's workshop." I learned the true essence of these words one nice spring day. She was cooking my favorite soup filled with veggies, meat and noodles. The aroma was heavenly and I couldn't wait to have a nice slice of yellow corn bread, I couldn't wait.

She asked what was I doing? I had been reading and one of the characters had stated that she was, "Bored." I really didn't have a concept of what that word meant, but when those words left my eleven year old mouth, I was in for a true eye opening experience.

Mother never stopped stirring the large pot. She had a smile on her lovely face and replied, "So you're bored." I immediately replied, "Yes, I am." Mrs. Ruth Ella said, "Go the back closet and get the broom, dust mop, dust pan, and dusting cloth and furniture polish and come back when you have everything.

I had no idea what was in store for me, but I was sure that some lesson was sure to follow. When I returned with the requested items, making two trips, she then said, "Since you're bored you may sweep the living room, your bedroom, our bedroom and your little brother's bedroom hardwood floors and you'll sweep the kitchen after we finish dinner.

The floors didn't need any sweeping or cleaning because they sparkled in the evening sun, then she told me to take the dust mop and pick up any remaining dust. After I completed that task I was to dust the furniture and I could also polish the furniture.

My mother said all of these commands with a smile on her face, not leaving the boiling pot. She did tell me that their were plenty more chores to do when I had finished. I could pull the weeds in the vegetable garden and the ones around her prized rose bushes. And once I had finished that, it would be time to set the table for dinner. I would later wash the dinner dishes. Get my bath and be ready for bed.

She then added I could help her polish the silver tea service tomorrow, and she wanted me to read the Book of Etiquette she had given me for Christmas. She added that she wanted a written summary, one page in length for the remainder of my spring break.

My next job would be to put the ice into the glasses for the ice tea. When we were younger we only drank water, milk, juice, fresh lemonade or ice tea with a sprig of mint from our garden. It was my duty to pick, wash and place the mint into the poured tea. We were not allowed to drink sodas, and if we had a soda we were given only half of a glass with ice.

After all of the tasks were completed, I didn't think of being "Bored" and never allowed that word to come into my mind or exit my mouth, at least where my mother could hear. I did my chores and found ways to be active. I am grateful for my lessons and the love I was given.

"LOVE YOUR HEART"

Grace Banks

The poetry reading group is a bit unique, with laughter, friends catching up, enjoying music, talking, having a prayer and watching the sunset while we wait for the others to arrive. Some of the writers share challenging stories after the reading had been completed. Each one of the authors has taught in different parts of the world. Their experiences reflect the events they have seen, heard or read about.

"No one said life was easy." There are choices in life of how we must deal with, challenges and how to make to respond to others in our lives. During the poetry reading, a topic is selected by someone and this in the highlight of the evening.

I enjoy being in George Bussey's space. There are twenty-two steps to walk up before you enter his lovely apartment near Trinity University in San Antonio, Texas. We eat delicious food and enjoy good poetry. When we all leave, there are twenty-two steps to walk down, plus five steps outside.

I have written these two essays to encourage the community to read, write and "To Love Your Heart." Improve you mind and get educated about heart disease. The fact that heart disease claims lives, taking the steps to a poetry reading is an excellent way to do both!

MY SISTER IS A POET

Grace Banks

My sister is a poet, and she keeps telling me to write something for the book. I keep telling her I did, but I must have thrown it away. We have formed a group of creative, people who get together to read and share their true stories or poetry. I am writing about these stories. One story is about Pat, a very nice lady, invited the group over for food and poetry. She prepared lasagna, a stew and a delicious salad. She even made two types of fresh bread.

My sister enjoys helping people with their writing. She comes in from work on her main job, when she arrives from her second job, she gets busy. When she gets set up, her fingers began busily working on her assignments. It is a shame we can't let her just write. She is a busy, busy woman. There are so many people who wouldn't get their story told if she hadn't given them her time. We love all our readers, my sister helps keep people motivated to do their best.

The best lesson we can teach people is to learn to shut their trap and watch the words that come out of it. It is better to do positive things and work hard as we were taught. Remember the words, "Do Right."

We love you sister dear, our writer.

WHAT DOES FREEDOM MEAN TO ME

Beatrice Anderson (Miss Bea)

A mind of freedom is like a blank canvas before an artist. That artist is the self within. The mind of one's self looks out through the eyes to capture a variety of the senses. The eyes of the soul sees only a much broader scope.

Yet, it is the blessed and privileged mind that has the ability to choose what it wishes to paint on the canvas; whether it captures in color or in black and white. The mind can travel distances far and near. It can move in all directions, sometimes seemingly all at once. The mind can leave and return, stay motionless. The mind can even choose the time where it wants to exist in and tarry alone independently and yes it is Oh! So, so free.

"SOUNDS FROM WITHIN"

Beatrice Anderson (Miss Bea)

What can be more beautiful and claiming than the sweet melodies from an old well-built organ, but the secret for the wonderful sound that is created by the gift of the player.

The organ is an instrument made of wood, strings and some metal. It has parts called pipes through which air is forced when the keys are pressed down. However, the sound ranges in various sizes, from large to small which in terms produce various pitches from very low to very high.

The organ also has parts called tabs that create a variety of tonal variations that sounds like a roaring train to angelic melodies. Now think there is a human being, who was created by God, the Master of all things, was uniquely designed with all of the necessary parts. When the human's mind and heart are in tune, with its maker feels the spontaneous urge to give expression.

The creature takes in air and through the movement of exhaling, created a vibration called sound. A melodious sound heard first by God on the inside; and secondly, by another human being with ears to receive the sound. Man is wonderfully and beautifully made. Did you hear the sounds? "Listen."

Inspired by Psalm 150

Praise the Lord!

Praise God in his heavenly dwelling;
praise Him in his mighty heaven!
Praise him for his mighty works;
praise him unequaled greatness!
Praise him with a blast of the trumpet,
praise him with lyre and harp!
Praise him with the tambourine and dancing;
praise him with stringed instruments and flutes!

Praise him with a clash of cymbals;
praise him with loud clanging of.
Let everything that lives sing praises to the Lord!

Praise the Lord!

*Holy Bible People's Parallel Edition King James
New Living Version Translation

After attending one of Sterling Houston's plays I told him,
"I love your work. When are you writing another one?"
He looked at me, smiled and replied,
"I'm waiting for you to write one."

CYNTHIA HINOJOSA

Dedicated to Helping Hurt and Abused Women

"...If only I had gathered enough courage to leave him,
I would not have gotten flowers...today. "
(I Got Flowers Today)
Pauline Kelly, Grace Ministry

"...I am a Domestic Violence Survivor. Jesus saved my life and I will continue to speak out against Domestic Violence and Abuse as an advocate to make a difference in the lives of thousands of victims, survivors and their families. I hope to make the difference and spread a ray of hope about this problem. As a spokesperson, I will prove to other victims that no matter what you've been through don't let the horrible past determine the outcome of your future."

"Shinning a spotlight on abuse will bring the serious issue that abusers should be held accountable for their actions. One voice makes ALL voices stronger."

Sincerely,
Cynthia Hinojosa

We must be our brother's and sister's keeper. The world is full of unhappiness and as a people we must look back and help those in need. Mrs. Hinojosa is a spokeswomen and advocate for teenage girls and women who have experience violence and abuse. Strive to do the best and spread some joy, truth and love into the world.

Antoinette V. Franklin
Managing Editor

ANGELIC

Karen McDonald (Angelic)

GO EGYPT, GO!

Mohammed El-Zomor

Cairo, Egypt- Nagib Mahfouz, a Nobel Prize winner, is one of the finest Egyptian writers of the 20th century. His many wonderful writings describe Egyptian society. One of the favorites, his "Cairo Trilogy," is considered an authentic description of the 25-year period from 1919 to 1944. In this three part series Mahfouz follows the life of one family, and through his characters, Saied Ahmed, his wife Amina, and their children, he portrays the common Egpytian people who experienced the remarkable history of those times. After reading this trilogy and watching the subsequent movie many times, with this in mind, I began walking through the city.

It is 1919. World War I had ended and the world is trying to heal the wounds left by the shedding of a river of blood, the loss of millions of soldiers and civilians from both sides. War is after all, a lose-lose game where everyone loses to some extent, but the winner is, the one who loses less. As I wander through this ancient city, everything seems as if history has stopped. Life is going on as usual, and by this I mean as it has for centuries: nothing has changed. It's the same as every day for hundreds of years. I go deeper and deeper into the city, seeing the old homes, houses built centuries ago with people still living there.

I am astonished. How could these people adapt to living here like this? But actually, there was no kind of adaptation. It was simple. These people have lived their life day by day with nothing called Tomorrow, nothing called The Future. So they could manage to keep on like that for centuries, as if it were yesterday.

In the 1920's, nothing has changed. People are doing their daily routine, living their life day by day. Still nothing called Tomorrow, nothing called The Future.

Now we are in the 1930's. Things have started to move a little bit forward. Our university graduates who got their education in the university and went to France and England for their Masters or PhD; began to see the differences between here and there and decided to do something. Egpyt at this time was under the custody of great Great Britain and a helpless king.

The late 30's was just the beginning of another phase of sorrow for mankind. We found ourselves in the middle of a war we didn't choose, a war we were forced to be in. So, when we thought that our salvation might be with Rommel, we marched the streets and shouted, "Go, Rommel, go!" But sorrowfully, Rommel lost his battle and we lost our hope and England won, so long live the king.

One fine day in 1952, I woke up to a noise from the street. It was something like a military parade. We weren't used to this kind of parade or any kind of parade, but this one was different. I don't know why, but I turned the radio on and found a speech being given by Sadat, a member of the Revolution Command Council. He was announcing the military coup against the British and the king. We couldn't believe what we were hearing, but we went to the streets crying, laughing and shouting. "Go Nasser, go!"

He was military, but we didn't care. We worked very hard and built new cities, a new civilization. At that time, the whole world was divided between two major powers, the East, the USSR, and the West, the USA. We had to choose one, but we not only chose neither, we started a non-proliferation movement when Nasser died, leaving a very heavy burden on Sadat, the man of war and peace.

We cried over Nasser, but the funeral turned into a rally for his successor.

"Go, Sadat, go!"

We gathered together and cried and laughed and even made jokes. Very strange are the Egyptians! In the darkest moments while crying, they turn these moments into funny stories and start to laugh.

Now it's 1982. Sadat has been assassinated. But we didn't stop. We followed after his vice-president, Hosni Mubarak, running in the streets and shouting. "Go Mubarak, go." and expecting him to make our dreams come true. His predecessors had done everything. They fought, they won and they made peace. In all that time, we didn't stop dreaming about Tomorrow, about the Future. But after 30 years with Mubarak, we still had nothing. We started again to live our lives day by day, with nothing called Tomorrow and nothing called The Future.

And then we remembered 1919. "No, no! Not again! We are not going back again." So January 25, 2011, we all went into the streets, shouting, "Go, Mubarak, go!" For the first time in history, we were calling for a president to leave.

Have you ever seen a baby 7,000 years old? Some will laugh and maybe some will cry but we need neither your smiles nor your sympathy or tears. We need your understanding. Give us time to learn. Over the centuries, we had taught the whole world every kind of knowledge, but not democracy because we had none. So let us fall down until we learn how to walk. Then we will learn how to run, and after that we can race with all of you. We only need time, so please give us a chance to try.

All we need is your understanding.

"The ability to read awoke inside me some long dormant craving to be mentally alive."

Autobiography of Malcolm X. 1994

"Don't take
criticism from anyone
who has never
written, produced or directed
anything."

Ezra Pound, Poet

"God gives us a song."

Ute Native American Proverb

REFERENCE PAGE

Abide in the Spirit of Change Impressive Jewels Cultural Magazine San Antonio, Texas Hayward Bethel, Francis Philips Lee and Antoinette V. Franklin 2012

Communities Creating Racial Equity Learning Exchange Auburn, New York 2008

Conquering The Stand-up Toilet: and other stories about living and teaching in Bulgaria" by Patricia Schwindt.

Holy Bible King James New Living Version Tyndale House Publishers, Inc. Wheaton, Illinois, 1997.

http:www.internet/cartergwoodson 2011

Impressive Jewels Cultural Magazine San Antonio, Texas 2009

La Voz de Esperanza for Peace and Justice San Antonio, Texas 2001

Love Letters to Jesus, 2012

Poet's Along the River San Antonio, Texas 1999

The Carver Literary Arts Society 2010 Anthology We Commemorate This Day, Xlibris, Bloomington, IN 2010

CONTRIBUTING AUTHORS

Set Your Compass to the Stars Anthology 2012

*****Denia Alvarado** was born in Costa Rica and migrated as a child to Milwaukee in the middle of winter to what seemed a magical world in white snow. From her attic window, she could see the steeple of St. Micheal's Church and the snow-covered roofs of the neighborhood houses. It was beautiful but lonely and strange. Nothing in this world seemed familiar or representative of who we were and she grew up feeling misplaced, dislocated. All of that changed when she found a poets group in Milwaukee who taught her to express herself in the written word, and that has made all the difference. She is grateful for this opportunity to share her thoughts with like-minded people. Denia has a degree in communications from Alverno College, Milwaukee, WI and a MA in TESL from University of Texas San Antonio, Texas.

*****Beatrice V. Anderson** is a native of Giddings, Texas. At an early age her family moved to Fort Worth, where she attended kindergarten and elementary school. She and her family moved again to La Mesa, Texas where she graduated from Blackshear High School. After graduation, she attended Texas Technical College, taking piano and voice. During her high school years and early college years, she sang in the church choir and played for various other churches.

Mrs. Anderson resides in San Antonio, Texas. She earned an AA in Business Administration from St. Philips College. She has retired from San Antonio Independent School District. She is active in both church and community affairs. Her favorite things are reading, music, traveling and community affairs. Her new found joy is inspirational writing.

*****Grace Banks** is the President of Impressive Jewels Cultural Magazine. She is a retired office manager of Sutton's Paradise Funeral Home. She believes in assisting the community and is an advocate for children and concerns for the elderly. She is a native of San Antonio, Texas. She is a member of the Friends of the Carver Library and presently is Grand Lady for the Ladies Auxiliary for St. Peter Claver. She was a contributing author in "The Carver Literary Arts Society Anthology 2010 We Commemorate This Day."

*Hayward Bethel, guest poet, author, motivational speaker is a poet and motivational speaker who lives in Austin, Texas. He always meets people with a smile and a positive antidote. He retired from civil service and became a poet and published Haywood's *Humor*. He often visits nursing care facilities and retirement communities to spread joy or share a joke with the residents to brighten their day and make them laugh their cares away. Hayward was a contributing author in *Abide in the Spirit of Change* published with Impressive Jewels Cultural Magazine 2012.

*George Bussey educator from Manhattan, New York, a new writer with an evolving voice.

*Aaron Deutsch is a graduate of the Texas State University MFA program where he was awarded his degree with distinction. He has been a lover of poetry since High School, when he read Seamus Heaney's "Bog People." He currently resides in San Antonio, Texas and is glad to have found a community of soulful, sophisticated writers to commune with. Of poetry, he feels it is responsible for recording the emotional consciousness of the people, both the ride we take down life's long roads, and the deer who get trapped in the headlights."

*Aaron Doyle poet is a 1976 graduate from The University of North Texas where he received a B. B. A degree in Business administration. He is the author of the recently published Poetry book "Open Vessel Writings: Taking Aim At Musing Over Matters Mete For Meaningful Or Mundane Meditations And Other Message Expressionisms." His upcoming poetry book titled "Journeys Through Divorce" is scheduled for release in September. Mr. Doyle is a motivational speaker, a humorist, a creator of crossword puzzle educational workbooks and a lyrical writer of country, gospel and blues songs.

*Antoinette V. Franklin sixth generation Texan began writing poetry and short stories at the age of six. She is the second daughter of Nathaniel and Ruth Ella Lara Franklin and the proud parent of Alexis Franklin. She has published 15 books, including poetry and autobiography and a book of short stories and a play. Ms. Franklin is owner or A Vicious Fox Literary Enterprises since 1992 and is Managing Editor of Impressive Jewels Cultural Magazine. She received an Honorable Mention from Writer's Digest in 2009 for *In the Mist of Struggle Stands a Woman published with Author House 2005, A Legacy To Leave Our Youth, Autobiography of John "Mule" Miles, Xlibris 2009, The Carver Literary Arts Society Anthology 2010,* Xlibris 2010, *Hot Women Needing A Man and other stories,* Publish America, *Abide in the Spirit of Change* and Impressive Jewels Cultural Magazine 2012. Her Motto: Always Follow Your Dreams. She has been a member of Delta Sigma Theta Sorority, Inc., since 1975. She has been a Pegasus Juror for the San Antonio Public Library, Office of Cultural Affairs and The Texas Commission of the Arts and now serves as President of the Friends of the Carver Library. Her educational background includes: BA Psychology Incarnate Word College 1978, MA Management Webster University 1990, MA Ed University Incarnate Word 1998.

*Cynthia Hinojosa is a survivor of domestic violence and has now become a spokeswoman against this horrible act against women, teenage girls and men. She is married to Rafael and is the proud parent of Richard, La Shondra, Darius, Au Breana and Jeremiah. She was Mrs. La Vernia 2010 and now become Mrs. Central Texas 2012. She is awaiting the release of her debut novel *Face of Deception* in the fall of 2012.

*Cortnee Mendoza, a rising new voice of the poetic world, is making a return to poetry with his publication in this anthology. In the past fifteen years, he has been published in various anthologies, placed in nationwide writing competitions and has authored *The Ivory Tower: Within and Outside,* a volume of his own work. Since the publication of this work, he has taken an unplanned hiatus from publishing his work, but never stopped writing, continuously being inspired by all of his experiences; abroad and domestic, learning from them and writing about them, so he has a lot of work accumulated. Early in his career, Mendoza was inspired by the works of

Spanish poet Federico Garcia Lorca, the Roman poet Gaius Valerius Catullus, and his own personal tendencies toward simplicity, brevity and vivid, dramatic imagery. He continues his practice of poetry with the hope of being a prolific poet whose work is appreciated and known in the diverse poetic community. He currently resides in San Antonio, Texas.

*Abdur-Rahim Muhammad, Imam was born and raised in New York's South Bronx, he became a poet and Muslim in college, an Imam in 1977. He made his hajj in 2000, visiting Mecca, Medina and Cairo Egypt. He has been blessed to speak before New York State Senate, the Oklahoma City Bombing victims, the 9/11 families and first responders. He is happy to see his work published in this anthology, now resides in San Antonio, TX.

*Linda Ruth Sheppard Oliver, native of San Antonio, Texas. She is a gifted actress, producer and director. She has been a program coordinator for the Boys and Girls Club and director of Adult and Community Education for the city of San Antonio. She is working on a PhD. in Metaphysics. Ms. Oliver is a loving mother, grandmother and a dear friend. Her main concerns are God, family and the community. She developed a program for St. Philips Community College that allowed GED students and their families to receive dictionaries and books for children to improve their reading. Her story *"When I Was Colored*...was published in La Voz de Esperanza for Peace and Justice March 2002.

*Patricia Schwindt was born and raised on the prairies of Kansas. She has raised children and followed her husband to work locations in Kansas, Arkansas, Missouri and finally Oklahoma. She accrued much fodder for the writing that would lay in her future. The next part of her life was the demise of her marriage in Oklahoma. She continued to raise her children and work as a newspaper reporter, writing about local education issues, police, city hall news and human interest topics. For a time, she had a regular column that focused on the famous and the ordinary, which she called *Emphasis: People*, was the editor of the weekly entertainment-religion section of the paper.

She began her college studies at Oklahoma State, working at the same time as the director of public relations for the growing local medical center.

She became well-known for her creative stories about hospital life and the current issues and technicality of medical care. She received an MA in teaching English as a Second Language. Her life now revolves around her children, her grandchildren and her work at the Defense Language Institute English Studies Section in San Antonio, Texas. She teaches in the Advanced English Studies Section, where she works with English teachers from around the world. Her main ambition is to be a "real" writer.

*Juanita (Sugar) Wilson is a devout Christian and loves singing God's praises. She tells her story of being dead three times and God breathed life back into her body to fulfill His word. Mrs. Wilson is a loving mother and grandmother. She is one of the guest poets and will be releasing her debut volume of poetry *Love Letters To Jesus* in the fall of 2012.

*Mohammed El-Zomor, simply "Zomor" to his friends, is a native speaker of Arabic and a long-time English Instructor for his country. He has studied advanced English at the American University of Cairo, and teaches at the American Middle East Institute (AMIDEAST) in Cairo.

Zomor has earned several diplomas from the Defense Language Institute (known as DLI) at Lackland AFB. Those courses include Basic American Language Culture, Methods and Culture Seminar, and ALPS II. He finds it exciting and challenging to write for purposes such as this collection, and he hopes to write more in the future.

⤙❖⤚

Contributing Photographer
*Rafael F. Domeyko is an underwater and sports photographer. He earned a Bachelors in Engineering and a Masters Degree in International Policy Studies. Rafael was raised and educated in California. He enjoys spending as much time in the water, sea or pool, as possible. His latest collection of the University of Incarnate Word 2012 National Championship Synchronized Swim Team is on display at UIW.

Contributing Artist

*Karen McDonald, Artist/Writer/Educator, has worked collaboratively on a variety of socially engaging, interdisciplinary projects. Coming from a long line of artist, her paintings have graced exhibitions in Tucson, Arizona, Miami and Florida - where she was a member of the One Ear Society. She now resides in San Antonio with her husband, who is also artist.